My Lady's So

by

Meryl M Williams

THE AUTHOR - MERYL M WILLIAMS Born 1966

Meryl was born in South Wales and studied the biological sciences before publishing a number of poetry books and a short story compilation. She is also the author of The Judge Jones Trilogy, utilising life experience to colour and add interest to her fiction. She enjoys giving poetry readings to friends, family and the general public and has contributed to local newsletters.

BY THE SAME AUTHOR

Mementoes in Verse
Reflections of Time
Doodles, Dog Ears and Ditties
A Boy's Anthem
Andrew's Amazing Odyssey and Other Stories
The Judge Jones Trilogy

MY LADY'S SOVEREIGN

CONTENTS LIST

I.   A Ruffian Returns

Episode 1 - News at Sunrise

A myriad of tiny stars light up the night sky but there's a
storm brewing, I can feel the chill wind flapping at my
cloak as I clutch the folds closer with numb fingers. The
herd are wallowing in the hot springs deep in the valley,
most of them are quietly resting but one has left the main
pack to go it alone. I think this particular swine is sick or
over weary like I'm feeling right now.

Getting here from the perilous mountain trail was
difficult and dangerous. Bandits hung in shrubbery along
the ancient pathways. I travelled by night, sleeping by day,
yearning for the shelter of Volcanic Vale as it was known
locally. The villagers were kind, giving bread, eggs and
milk in exchange for a suckling pig. They were grateful for
news of the outside world although it's been many moons
since I left the township. They asked for my name which I
always gave them.

"Bladud" I would say, fearing reprisals, although it
seemed that in these remote parts I was mercifully
unknown. I'd been on the road for many weeks, my feet
blistered and calloused from the stones of the rough
mountain tracks. Finally I'd bought this herd of swine from
a farmer for more than they were worth but he gave me an
aging boar for good measure.

"I was born under a lucky star" I cried when the first
piglets were born. I found myself giving the pigs names,
talking to them as old friends and learning how to treat their
ailments. From a traveling pedlar I bought a tool to clean

out their hooves which was a satisfying job leading to grunts and snorts of relief.

"Swine seem to be very patient animals", I mused on that chilly night of only a crescent moon.

I slept for just a few hours wrapped in my cloak, under a makeshift shelter by the edge of the swamp until the sun's rays were beginning to lighten the Eastern sky. A tinkling noise afar off suggested the traveling pedlar was heading my way once more.

"It's company", I thought, washing my face in a wayside pool of water. The pedlar was in a mood to talk, he spoke of a great army coming that way after three full moons.

"A battle", I answered, "but where, good pedlar? Surely not near a swamp".

"On yonder hilltop", the pedlar persisted as he pointed to a place I'd not long passed.

I looked at his pack of trinkets and bought a comb for my beard with a few of my last coins.

"Thank you my friend" I cried "for the news and the trinket. But where do you go from here?"

The pedlar, a clean shaven man, squinted at the rising sun then faced away from it.

"I go towards the setting sun to new villages and people with a strange tongue of whom I've heard a little. But you my friend will need all your wits about you to protect your herd. A marching army is a hungry army and I have seen enough butchery in these parts".

He set off, his pack on his shoulders, bent a little then straightening up. He moved swiftly westward without the aid of his stick which he swung as he chirruped to the birds.

Episode 2 - With Hindsight

I watched the phases of the moon with more than my usual concentration. The villagers showed scant interest, expressing the opinion that nothing exciting ever came their way. I bought my usual supplies, picking acorns from the woods for my herd to feed on. The third full moon was high in the sky when I heard a rattling and the crunch of wheels as I walked back to the swamp to join my herd. I moved my cloak to conceal my face as the drover called out to me.

"Swineherd, have you seen a prince of the blood royal in these parts?" He pulled up, leaning down to move away my hand.

"No blood prince have I seen, kind Sir", I croaked, my hood drawn close over my ears. The drover looked suspicious but noting my calloused feet and humble apparel he soon went on his way. I couldn't sleep that night as the past came flooding back. I'd left my father's royal court, fleeing to this seemingly safe haven to save my miserable life which was sought by the cruel Earl of Woden, a love rival. I'd left my beautiful lady Athelstan with a Sovereign as pledge but the pedlar had no news of her when last I tried to find out.

I berated myself that lonely night by the hot springs. I'd left Athelstan defenceless to protect my own skin with only my aging father to look out for her. I craved news as the full moon gave way to the rising sun but then I climbed the nearest hillside. Facing East I saw a glint of armour and chainmail just as the pedlar promised. An army was marching, heading West but veering South of my swamp.

The army came to a halt as their brightly coloured pennants fluttered in the cooling breeze. I gazed open mouthed until I could see the Royal coat of arms of my own

3

house with those of my Lady Athelstan. As I gazed across the landscape, members of the cavalry dismounted and it seemed to me that the army was preparing to camp for the night. I remembered the pedlar's warning and reviewed my herd. Two messengers bearing my father's pennant strode down the hillside, coming to greet me very swiftly. I drew my cloak fast around me and stood up.

"Kind friend" said one, "my honoured lord the king seeks food for his army. We have money and can pay you well". This last was so unexpected I stopped hiding and flung back my hood.

"Sir, my herd is at my honoured king's disposal. All I ask is that you leave one sow and the boar for me. No payment will I take except that of knowing I serve my king".

The two messengers paused then spoke to one another.

"He has a familiar voice and regal bearing". Then they spoke to me.

"You will be rewarded by dining at the king's table this night", said the first man. "Can you round up your herd, bringing them to our camp". Then the messengers departed while I persuaded the hogs and sows wallowing in the hot springs to leave this comfortable swamp never to return.

Episode 3 - My Lady's Sovereign

My Lady Athelstan sat quietly on an oak chest while a team of well organized pages put up her tent with tents for her waiting women.

"Job done" cried the foreman, then Athelstan rose to enter her marquee as the boxes were brought in behind her.

"Fetch me my jewellery casket if you will Lady Anca" she asked and the casket was brought to her. Lady Athelstan chose a golden brooch with a ruby adorning its clasp then from underneath her other jewels she opened a red velvet trinket bag. Out of the bag she took a golden Sovereign, shiny, polished and well loved. "His pledge to me that he would return yet six full moons have I seen without word. The money would buy us comforts, pay for food as the army eats so much or buy medicine for my sick mother back home. Perhaps I should finally part with this coin, accept the hand of the Earl of Woden and bring peace to our two warring factions". The bugle sounded so Athelstan rose with the Sovereign in her hand.

"I'll do it", she said to Lady Anca, "please honourable page, take this Sovereign to the king, telling him he can pay the swine herd. For myself I can stomach no rich food tonight and will retire early".

The king sat at the trestle table as servers brought in roast hogs with other dishes gathered that day. He studied the Sovereign with great curiosity, having a mind to ask Lady Athelstan where it came from. But he didn't want her to change her mind so he spoke to the page asking for the swine herd to come to the top table. The disguised Prince Bladud came forward, wondering if the Sovereign was his own.

"My Lady Athelstan begs you to accept this token to thank you for providing such a sumptuous banquet this night", King Wolfric declared, holding out the coin. Prince Bladud hesitated, very reluctant to take back the coin, then he knelt down and uncovered his head.

"Father", he said gently, "no payment is required".

II.   A Transforming Power

Episode 1 - My Lord Earl

"Clearly", cried the Earl of Woden, astride a bench before the king, "this man is an imposter. See the corns on his hands and feet, his untidy, unkempt apparel, his unshaven locks. I will not believe that this is our missing prince."

"Gave you this coin to my Lady Athelstan?" asked King Wolfric.

"I did", replied Prince Bladud, "and I have tested her patience to the limit. But if she chooses my rival in love, a lady should never be forced. I would submit but ask her how she came by this coin." Lady Anca disturbed Athelstan as she reposed on a couch of feather pillows.

"The King's Grace wishes to speak with you", said Anca apologizing. Obedient to the man she had long looked up to as a father, Athelstan rose, drew her cloak about her and walked to the marquee where the king was dining.

"The coin is indeed from Bladud", said she, "but I do not recognize this dishevelled ruffian. My mother who lies sick at home has nursed Bladud from a child. She said he has a distinguishing mark on his right knee once won in a fall from his horse." Prince Bladud bowed low to his lady and spoke in a voice she recognized.

"If you permit me, my lady, I will clean myself up. I have slept beneath the stars for six moons but am truly sorry. The mark you speak of is there for all to see if I fling back my cloak. My royal tunic beneath is quite short." My Lady Athelstan saw the mark and exclaimed as she held out the golden Sovereign.

"As you have returned to us, sound of body and mind, take this gold coin which I've kept for so long. Consider it to be my only dowry as I have nothing. But if I give myself to you my whole county will fight the Earl, can you settle this matter in one armed combat to save all our peoples?" Once again Prince Bladud bowed low to his lady as the Earl of Woden flung his gauntlet at Bladud's feet.

"Choose your weapons", sneered the Earl as Bladud picked up the glove, replacing it on the king's table. Then Bladud asked the king if he could make himself clean and presentable as befits the ladies. Wolfric consented offering his armoury of swords to both combatants. Bladud chose with care, promising to meet the Earl at sunrise the next morning. Lady Anca bid Lady Athelstan to try and get some rest then the whole company disbanded for the night.

Episode 2 - Chieftains in Combat

Grey skies with a light drizzle heralded the dawn as a clean shaven Prince Bladud, with neatly trimmed hair, appeared before King Wolfric who finally recognized his son. An area was marked out for the combat and at a signal from the bugler battle commenced. To start with it looked as though the Earl would have the upper hand as his sword thrusts rained down on Bladud. But the younger man rallied, finally bringing Woden to his knees. The prince's sword was resting gently against the Earl's chest while the crowds bayed for blood.

Prince Bladud drew his sleeve across his brow then thrust his sword into the ground.

"A fair victory", conceded the Earl as King Wolfric approached.

"My son", cried the king "what prize shall I grant you?"

"Let our two warring factions be at peace in my lifetime", Bladud proclaimed to the assembled throng. Then he helped the Earl of Woden to his feet.

"It is my Lady Athelstan's choice", said Bladud quietly as she held out her hand to the prince. As a victory March was played on the bugle a commotion was heard amongst the crowds. Lady Anca appeared with a young boy whom she presented first to the king and then to the Earl of Woden.

"Your Grace, this is your child", said Anca, lowering her eyes as she curtsied to the Earl.

Unbeknown to the crowd the Earl was particularly skilled at training pages, heralds and other young people in his entourage. He asked the young boy about his favourite lessons and leisure pursuits. Then Woden turned to Anca, marveling at this miracle.

"Mistresses I've had aplenty but no sign of a child"; he sounded bemused then asked the boy's age.

"Brava is five years old next month", then Anca smiled and spoke to the king.

"My son is the delight of my eye while his Sire has waged war against my adopted country all my living memory".

"A double wedding" the king declared regally, "but first a feasting".

Episode 3 - Stitching for a Queen

Five years after the double wedding of Prince Bladud and the Earl of Woden to their respective ladies, the skies were dark with a cold wind. King Wolfric was unwell, he was delirious with a fever that he'd picked up campaigning in the west. Lady Athelstan fetched her own mother to assist her in nursing him as the Dowager Duchess had recovered from a similar malady.

With the king it seemed more serious, he had difficulty sleeping and spoke at random about his late wife who had died when Prince Bladud was quite young. Lady Athelstan now had a child of her own, but she attended King Wolfric without fear. Then after a long day she spoke to her husband of the king's deterioration and Bladud was shown into his father's room. Wolfric rested with his hand on Bladud's arm as the king breathed heavily in an ancient blessing. Then the king closed his eyes for the last time.

"The king is dead, long live the king", announced the heralds followed by a proclamation of a time of mourning before the date was set for Bladud's coronation. Brava, now a page, was sent by his parents to greet the new king.

"My honoured liege", he declared, standing his ground before King Bladud and Queen Athelstan, "my lady mother has requested a new tapestry to celebrate the coronation. She would like it to depict all the beauties of our two counties with portraits of all the royal family in fine stitching. My father has decreed that the poor people of Woden's Dyke should have a part to play in its design".

"I accept your commission", replied King Bladud. "We know that your esteemed mother is a fine seamstress just as the Earl is a skilled teacher. I would like to ask that they oversee the work after we have held a design competition that all our heralds will proclaim". Brava bowed low and swiftly returned on horseback to his parents telling them of the good news.

Countess Anca declared at supper the next day that she had enjoyed a very constructive morning. A vast number of people, ordinary men and women, had come in large numbers with samples of their sewing to show her.

"There are some wonderful examples", she told them, "do present your best designs while our scribes take down the ideas". Brava asked his father who would be judging the competition?

"Maybe we will choose a team effort", answered the Earl. "I think we need an entry from the under elevens', what say you, Brava?" The Earl's son was delighted, approving of this idea by telling all his friends on the lower tables.

III.   The Temple of Oak

Episode 1 - Princess Auspicia

Many designs were put forward for the new royal tapestry while preparations for the coronation of King Bladud and his Queen went ahead. A holiday was announced by the heralds with a feast for all people throughout both counties, now at peace.

The king and queen were to be crowned in the Temple of the gods of peace right in the heart of Bladud's home township, where Athelstan had also grown up. Brava had been chosen out of all the pages to carry Bladud's crown on a purple cushion, while the Earl and Countess of Woden were to be in attendance.

The day of the coronation dawned and servants came to assist the King and Queen into their royal robes. But little Princess Auspicia had not risen for breakfast or entered the gardens to greet the dawn as she so often did. Athelstan removed her gilded cloak, saying to her husband that she would join him later in the Temple, then she followed the nurse to Auspicia's bedside. The young princess was listless, awake but had rejected her favourite breakfast of oats with pomegranate seeds.

"The little lady had been to the barn where the swine are", grieved the nurse wringing her hands. "I turned my back for one second but Auspicia is a bit wild I fear".

"It's a tummy upset from eating the acorns the swine feed on", Athelstan reassured the nurse, "but baby Auspicia do you not want to see Daddy crowned? One day it will be your turn and it's high time we hired a tutor to teach you deportment". But little Auspicia buried her head under the

11

blankets and wouldn't budge. Queen Athelstan gave Nurse Daphne instructions to offer the young lady her lunch at midday then hastened away to the coronation.

The Temple of the gods of peace was built entirely of good English Oak. The worshipping chamber was high with great tree trunk sized pillars decorated with carvings of animals and birds. For the inner sanctuary there were golden eagles carved in wood and overlaid with real gold leaf. The gold had been brought to the Temple from lands afar to the west. King Bladud joined his wife and they took their places on Golden thrones for the ceremony. Bugles played a triumphal March then the royal harpist made sweet music as the couple received their crowns from Brava and the Temple authorities. The Temple had been adorned with branches of oak and mistletoe so after the coronation the royal couple exchanged a kiss.

Queen Athelstan slipped away from the feasting to check on her daughter but there was no improvement. Nurse Daphne had prepared a delicious lunch of all the princess's favourite foods, had read stories and plumped up the pillows but Auspicia was still fretful and refusing to eat. The queen was now seriously alarmed, so she sent messengers to her husband and asked the page to fetch the High Priest.

Episode 2 - The Heir Apparent

"Brava" called the Earl of Woden to his son. "Should anything happen to Princess Auspicia, you will be next in line to the throne as ancient laws prevent me from inheriting in our neighbouring County. But you are the next heir through your beloved mother who is more royal than ever Wolfric was". Before Brava could reply, a tinkling noise was heard in the grounds of their home and the young boy went to investigate. It was the pedlar, still with his pack of trinkets before him as he held his staff of wood.

"Young man", said the pedlar softly, "do you desire to be king? I have medicines that will secure the succession for you as Princess Auspicia is not bound to live. Take this bottle of elixir as the Queen trusts you. All I ask in return is that once you are crowned you tear down the heathen Temple of the gods of peace, replacing it with a new stone Church in honor of a vengeful God from the East".

The pedlar departed leaving Brava holding a small clay bottle with a cork stopper. Brava sniffed at the elixir and thought to himself, "it can't do any harm, it's only cheap wine so possibly it might do some good. But the king of our two counties has no power to attack the sacred Temple so he can't win on that score".

Brava ordered for his pony to be saddled, rode hard through the morning, then reached the royal Palace by noon. Queen Athelstan was waiting quietly while the High Priest burned incense and mumbled prayers at Auspicia's bedside. Brava presented the Pedlar's elixir then fled as Nurse Daphne administered the wine to the little Princess. Auspicia drank every drop then fell into a deep sleep but the nurse was very fearful of getting blamed if anything went wrong so she smashed the clay bottle into pieces and buried them. Queen Athelstan called for her husband but her only child slipped away that afternoon and Bladud did not as yet know his enemy.

"We will have other children", he comforted his distraught wife, "but we will continue work on the tapestry as Auspicia's likeness has already been stitched."

Episode 3 - A County Mourns

Princess Auspicia lay in state at the Temple of the gods of peace for three days then her body was transported by wagon to a sacred burial site. The hills around Volcanic Vale fell silent as the little body was committed to earth. King Bladud was disturbed in his reverie by the pedlar who, after offering words of sympathy, suggested medicine to assist the queen in conceiving again.

"Nay, good pedlar. It is only cheap wine that can do no good. But the pain I feel is as nothing to the pain of being disenfranchised. I know not your name or your story, so tell me, are you from the West?"

"You guess correctly", replied the pedlar, "for my name is Cennen and I am your kinsman through your late father's illegitimate half brother who was my father. But I am not high minded, seeking only a pedlar's way of life. The new faith is sweeping the country from the West, the old traditions are being replaced with kindness and mercy yet the wrath of the new God is mighty".

"We will speak of this when mourning is over", the king answered, then he joined Queen Athelstan and returned to their wooden Palace with its thatched roof. The King and Queen mourned their daughter for six full moons, as Queen Athelstan retired from public duty. Countess Anca supervised the progression of the tapestry with beautiful stitched scenes of the countryside surrounding Woden's Dyke and pictures of the key figures in Bladud's family tree. No picture or likeness of the late king's half brother was included but, by authority of King Bladud, a portrait was stitched of Cennen the pedlar with his pack and wooden staff.

Brava went to the Temple of the gods of harvest and fulfilment to burn incense, to view the burgeoning tapestry and to speak to his tutor Arasmus.

"Do you understand the new faith?" asked Brava, "and will the good pedlar inherit the throne?"

"The queen is young and most likely to have another child", answered wise Arasmus, "but if you are next in line you will need to apply yourself to your lessons without worrying about matters of state. As to the new faith, it's a craze in the West that is unlikely to catch on in Woden's Dyke. The gods of fulfillment have sent a sign, Athelstan will conceive. Don't forget you are your father's heir too, let's focus on geography as the Earl of Woden is planning a treatise with the West".

IV.   In Aid of Trade

Episode 1 - The Good Pedlar

Cennen the pedlar returned once more to the West as Woden's Dyke prepared for the unveiling of the new tapestry. During the time of mourning for Princess Auspicia, Cennen retreated to a small island off the Western peninsula, where he was cared for by a community of brothers. The pedlar bought ointments for his calloused feet, rested his body and wondered how the queen was faring.

"Good pedlar", asked the brothers, "do you intend to contest the throne with your lineage?"

"Am I fit to lead after many moons on the road?" Cennen asked the brothers. "My father was never acknowledged by King Wolfric who never told Bladud about me nor asked to see me. I have no army, have never led in battle but my father was older than Wolfric which makes me the rightful heir. I would remember this community with great generosity but I need your help. On his deathbed my father secretly married my mother. If you can prove my legitimacy I have a better right even than Bladud's heir and Brava is still a young boy".

"Such a document is already in existence", claimed one brother, "it was taken for safety to the fortified township where Bladud lives. It is hidden away in a secret closet at the High Priest's domicile but we daren't risk stealing it for fear of eternal punishment".

"This document is mine by rights", insisted Cennen "and I will find it. Thank you brother Scriptus".

Cennen watched the phases of the moon until mourning for Auspicia was over, then he returned to the mainland by coracle, arriving in Woden's Dyke at sunrise. The tinkling noise which heralded his arrival had ceased as he had removed enough of his trappings to appear noiselessly. At the Temple of the gods of peace, deep in the heart of Bladud's home township, the High Priest was easily overcome by the strong narcotic in Cennen's elixir. The pedlar found the vellum document he sought in a wooden casket beneath the very throne that King Wolfric and later King Bladud had been seated on for their respective coronations.

"The irony of it all", mused Cennen as he fled to Volcanic Vale to sell his cheap wine and trinkets, while recruiting a band of fighting men.

"We're not convinced", grumbled the farm hands. "Your grandfather may have been King Wolfric's father but who was your grandmother? It's a tenuous claim hardly worth risking our lives for, King Bladud has an army and you would forfeit your own life if you assassinated the king. The High Priest lies dead in a drunken stupor, we fear the anger of the gods of war, and we would be butchered".

Episode 2 - Brava Sets Sail

Brava was thirteen years old when his father deemed him to be old enough for a diplomatic mission beyond the Western sea.

"You see Brava", explained Arasmus, "Woden's Dyke produces the finest wool whereas Ireland can trade in linen and beef. Consider this a peacetime activity as Queen Athelstan expects her second child, which will be delivered by the expert Nurse Daphne. King Bladud will be blessed with an heir under whom we must all surely prosper. Do not repine then but set sail in fair weather to do your father's bidding".

Brava rode on horseback to the sea port from where he would set sail and inspected his ship the Countess Anca which was being loaded with bales of purest wool. His tutor Arasmus had given much needed advice but the ship, made of leather over a wooden frame, had a full crew. The Captain invited Brava to inspect the ship and crew while they discussed plans to take harbour at Donne Laoghaire on the Irish coast.

"It's a fair South-east wind will get us there directly", cried the bold Captain, "but we have a fine body of oarsmen should the wind fail".

Brava spent one night with the crew in hammocks below deck then as the sun rose the Captain yelled orders to prepare for sail. But as the canvas sails were being unfurled a horseman called out from the shore, asking to be let on board. Brava came on deck to hear the news that Queen Athelstan had given birth to a fine, healthy boy and all of the Royal family were rejoicing.

"Send our congratulations and all good wishes to the mother and baby", declared Brava who gave the messenger a shilling for his trouble then at last the wooden and leather boat set sail across the Western sea towards the lands of Ireland.

As the good ship Countess Anca sailed into harbour at Donne Laoghaire, the oarsmen brought her closer then Brava landed from a small coracle and felt Terra firma beneath his feet once more. Mists covered the surrounding Wicklow Mountains, the shore was strewn with pebbles but Brava was greeted by a messenger from the Burghers of Dublin city who then invited him to inspect their cattle.

"I bring bales of our finest English wool", cried Brava to the gathered throng as Captain O'Driscoll gave the order to unload. As a cold wind blew in from inland the Burghers accompanied Brava to the thriving marketplace where he saw bales of fine, woven linen cloth as well as cattle and sheep.

Episode 3 - On Fairest Isle

While Brava was negotiating a good deal for the bales of wool entrusted to his care, his adversary Cennen the pedlar had bolted once again to the community of brothers on their beautiful island off the Western coast. Cennen went this time to find sanctuary and safety on the orders of King Bladud after the people of Volcanic Vale had sent word of Cennen's planned insurrection. The brothers questioned the pedlar, then Brother Scriptus wrote to Bladud to say they could find no reason to believe his claim to the throne was valid.

"We fear for the good pedlar's mind", wrote Brother Scriptus in his best round hand on a piece of vellum. "He has been advised to rest his weary limbs while he finds new life tending the kitchen gardens. We do not know for how long he will enjoy this new peace of mind".

King Bladud sent gifts of wine, wool and gold to the brothers with a message of good will then spoke to his queen. Since the birth of the new prince, Queen Athelstan had been listless with fatigue. She spent her days eating sweetmeats while listening to the Royal harpist playing mournful airs. When Bladud was shown into the queen's chamber he found Nurse Daphne trying to settle the new baby after a feed.

"My dear, we haven't yet named our new baby", the king patiently reminded his wife.

"What is your name, young man?" Athelstan asked the bard who paused in his sorrowful strumming.

"It is Jeremy your Grace", he answered her.

"That settles it then", cried Athelstan, "the child shall be called Jeremy and yours shall be the honour of teaching him to play and sing".

King Bladud dismissed the harpist then spoke to Athelstan firmly.

"My dear", he started again, "I entreat you to rouse yourself. You have gained weight, your beauty is all but gone. What good can all this lying around do you?" Queen Athelstan sank back on her feather pillows breathing heavily then finally spoke.

"Nurse Daphne takes excellent care of the child", she gasped, "while you busy yourself with affairs of state and war in the Western lands. There is nothing for me to do and the bard gives me comfort".

"Athelstan you have the keys to the spice cabinet, you could organize the cooks, we could entertain. There is plenty to do". Her husband entreated her but frustrated at her lack of enthusiasm he grew angry. "If the situation gets any worse I must put you away from me", he threatened then left the room. His queen moved to gaze at her sleeping infant, then shed bitter tears as she spoke to Nurse Daphne.

"My beautiful, lost princess", sobbed Athelstan, "how do I know this one won't fare the same?"

"Tush!" exclaimed Daphne, "a fine healthy boy. He will grow to be a king one day. It needs a good night's rest then everything will seem better".

V.   Jeremy the Bard

Episode 1 - Woden's Pride

Brava traded fairly, ordering the loading of his ship with livestock and as much pure, Irish linen as the ship would hold. He returned to Woden's Dyke to be greeted by delighted parents and a proud tutor. Brava questioned Arasmus about the new prince, trying to hide his own disappointment at being displaced from inheriting the throne.

"Do not deal with rumours", instructed the tutor when Brava asked after the queen. "She is taking the waters at Volcanic Vale while baby Jeremy is cutting his first teeth. They are all fine now so the plan is to dictate your report on your first trade mission then we will set it out on vellum. Have you been practicing your fine italics?"

While Brava wrote a meticulous report on his trading of wool for livestock and linen, King Bladud rode across the county to speak with the Earl of Woden about a proposed war with Western lands. But to the surprise of the king, the Earl did not favour war.

"No", he declared most decisively, "My liege I feel strongly enough to withhold my support. The people of the West have made a treaty, their messengers speak of floods and disease that have worn them out of any planned insurrection and Brother Scriptus writes from the South-West of Ceredigion to report a big increase in the number of people appealing to his community for aid. You are a merciful and just king, these people need ploughshares not weapons. Like yourself I have sent the good brothers gold, wine and linen to make shirts for those who are the most

21

needy. The people of the West have been subdued by natural forces beyond their control in a way that could have been any one of us, they are sorely afflicted".

King Bladud rode down the hill side to bring the news to his Queen who was quietly teaching her bard to read. Young baby Jeremy, the bard's namesake, crooned sweetly from his crib while Nurse Daphne prepared a lotion to ease the baby's tooth ache.

"Such sweet domestic felicity", declared Bladud sitting on a wooden chair, "but what are you reading?"

"It's a song I wrote myself", replied the bard, "which Her Grace has put down on vellum for me. I know the letters but sometimes they don't make out what I want them to say and the Queen has made me a fair copy. If you permit me I will sing this song which was inspired by Countess Anca's fabulous tapestry".

Episode 2 - Music to Soothe

A time of mourning was once again declared as Queen Athelstan's mother, the Dowager Duchess passed away.

"A life well lived", sighed the Queen as her dear departed mother was laid to rest alongside the much missed Princess Auspicia. The burial barrow overlooked Volcanic Vale so the queen took a walk to the village to meet some of the people. Matrons from the thriving local farms brought gifts of cake and posies of wild flowers which Athelstan accepted graciously. The Royal baby Prince Jeremy was much admired so the queen smiled sweetly as she climbed back into her carriage for the journey back to the Royal Palace.

Queen Athelstan was finding new life in her interest of teaching Jeremy the bard to read and write. He was making good progress but the Royal baby was left increasingly to the care of Nurse Daphne who took very good care of him. King Bladud was still anxious to subdue the people of the Western lands, as he was always conscious of their threatened insurrections of old. Brother Scriptus wrote again to say that Cennen the Pedlar had made a full confession to the assassinations of both Princess Auspicia and the High Priest and was attempting to leave the community to seek his fortune overseas.

"He must face trial" ordered King Bladud, sending soldiers to the brothers with instructions that Cennen be brought before the highest court of two counties. But Cennen was weak in body and spirit, the brothers advised that the pedlar would not understand the gravity of the charges against him and was unlikely to survive the journey.

"We are deprived of justice", insisted the distraught king, "put the pedlar to the sword". The soldiers stormed the manor house where the brothers lived but found no pedlar; one soldier found Cennen's abandoned coracle resting on the mainland side of the Channel suggesting he'd made the perilous journey from their island unaided.

On a dark, stormy night in the depths of winter just as Prince Jeremy was learning to walk and talk, his father the king decided to try once more to enlist the support of the Earl of Woden in suppressing the people of the Western lands. Before King Bladud set off to speak to his old rival he searched his oak chest to find the Sovereign that was Queen Athelstan's only dowry.

"We will see if Woden can be bought if reason won't prevail", argued Bladud to himself as he called for his fleetest horse.

Thunder claps hailed from the skies as jagged lightning flashed around the king but nothing deterred him as he rode alone along the ancient pathways that led to Woden's Dyke. His route took him through woodland causing him to slow but there were no stars or moon to guide him. A startled badger leapt away from the thundering horse's hooves, the horse shied and King Bladud was flung out of the saddle into the cold mud.

Villagers came into the woods to gather mushrooms at dawn and found a man's body lying on the forest floor. Nearby his horse stood patiently while drinking from a wayside pool of water. One young woman recognized the Royal ensign on the dead man's tunic after having seen the badge on Queen Athelstan's carriage just weeks before. But they did not at first realize that the dead horseman was in fact King Bladud.

"He must be buried somewhere", they argued amongst themselves, "such a valuable horse too. We could sell him at Woden's mart but someone should tell the Earl."

Episode 3 - The Dowager Queen

Countess Anca was chosen by her husband to bring the news of King Bladud's death to Queen Athelstan and an honest villager restored the golden Sovereign still in its original red, velvet bag. The Dowager Queen roused herself into preparing the most respectful yet lavish funeral and King Bladud was laid with his mother-in-law on the same hillside as his only daughter. The elders of the Temple approached Her Grace offering her the Regency until Prince Jeremy would be old enough to inherit the throne.

"Death, nothing but death", mused Athelstan but the ambitious bard took liberties with her as she wrung her hands. Taking hold of her arm he spoke in a menacing whisper.

"We can marry now", he urged, "you are free. We can leave the child to the care of your nurse and travel. I will show you the big cities, shower you with every luxury, get away from Woden's Dyke". The Dowager Queen would almost have been taken in but the bard had been chewing wild garlic and Athelstan flinched. As she recoiled, he saw her reaction and stepped back.

"We will consider", she said regally as she stood behind the couch, "but in the meantime I must meet with the elders and the Earl of Woden to discuss the Regency as people pay their respects to the late king. We have affairs of State and may not be able to just walk away. Perhaps you can write an Ode to the Prince who will be a king one day". The bard bowed low and left her chamber as the Earl of Woden was admitted.

"My liege", exclaimed Woden, "I seek your honest advice. The late king had once approached me for support in dealing with the rebellious people of the Western Lands. Should I take arms as Brother Scriptus writes of unrest?"

Queen Athelstan moved to recline on her couch and invited the Earl to sit near her.

"Not by my counsel", she answered, "as I always felt that there were genuine grievances. We have taxed them heavily many times, in warfare they always have the upper hand so perhaps we should trade, as with Brava and Ireland".

"I hear you", Woden continued, "but their wool is high quality, their meat much sought after. What would we offer as a bargaining product?"

"We have used their wool for our very own celebratory tapestry. We have used our own, locally produced dyes to create an item of luxury that would grace any draughty, Western longhouse. We have expert local needlewomen, could we not offer these sorts of items using Western wool?" The Queen concluded then spoke again. "Do they embellish their Temples?" she asked.

The Earl of Woden thought then replied by drawing in the sand.

"They build their new churches from rock", he explained, "and decorate the entrances with carvings using a hammer and chisel. Within the church is a table with lamps of Western gold from the north of the country".

"Gold?", queried Athelstan sitting bolt upright.

"Yes", insisted Woden, "it's very valuable and pure. But costly when we merely farm sheep and cattle".

"I want an end to more bloodshed", asserted the Queen firmly. From a chain at her waist she unfastened the small, velvet bag then held out her special gold Sovereign. "Take the coin", she ordered, "and pay the needlewomen to make fancy goods to sell across the border. Send your son Brava to me for perhaps after the success of his mission to Ireland he would like to take this on. It is our Royal command". The Earl bowed low and left her to seek out his family.

VI.   Prosperity Flourishes

Episode 1 - Brother Libris

As the sun set over Fairest Isle, a lapping of waves sounded loud against the quiet of the evening. Cennen the pedlar disembarked from his coracle which he moored to a stump of wood kept just for his use. He'd been sleeping rough, was dishevelled and unkempt, only returning to the brothers when he could no longer forage for himself in the mainland woods. He crept silently through the kitchen gardens startling Brother Libris at prayer in the community chapel.

"Your life is forfeit if you do not face trial", advised the brother, "do you understand the gravity of the charges against you?"

"I am the rightful king of Woden's Dyke", asserted Cennen, "I have the document that proves my claim". Brother Libris sighed then directed the pedlar to the refectory where supper was available. The brother found his colleague Scriptus and asked for a letter to the Earl of Woden.

"For if we do not hand in this fugitive from justice, we may face dire penalties ourselves", admitted Brother Libris. Brother Scriptus had a sudden idea and consulted the community herbalist before writing his letter. On his best advice, the herbalist bought a bottle of Cennen's elixir then poured it into a cup. The cheap wine was deep red but had little aroma. "It's elderberry wine but the tang suggests deadly nightshade", explained the herbalist who spat his mouthful into the kitchen conduit then rinsed his mouth with good wine.

"A strong man might not be affected, but it was enough to kill a young, sickly child and an older, temperate man. Neither would be used to strong drink". Brother Scriptus took notes then composed his letter to Earl Woden. "We feel", dictated the Earl in his short communication back to the brothers, "that if the miscreant is too sick to stand trial, then let him be held under house arrest with restricted movements. His coracle must be destroyed and his trinket pack be forfeit to the Crown".

A young horseman took Cennen's trinket pack on the long journey from Fairest Isle to Woden's Dyke for the Earl to destroy all the bottles of nasty elixir. Countess Anca suggested selling the golden trinkets to raise money which was sent back to the brothers for the poor. Meanwhile Cennen himself continued to tend the kitchen gardens where he was not allowed outside the confines of the community. He still rambled in his mind but the herbalist kept Cennen under close supervision to ensure he made no more potions.

Episode 2 - A King in Training

The Dowager Queen lay on her velvet couch, trying to interest herself in a plate of vegetable crudite while Jeremy the bard strummed on a new fangled instrument - his latest acquisition which he called a lute. Nurse Daphne brought in the young prince who tugged at his mama's sleeve.

"Mother!" he shouted, "we're going to be King of all England". His weary mama took his hand and smiled.

"Yes my dear", she said absently.

"But I would like to use my middle name which is stronger for a King. So from now on Mother I must insist you call me Jeremy Lear Brent or Lear for short. I will be bold and fearless and make a treatise with the West like my neighbour in Woden's Dyke".

Queen Athelstan roused herself and spoke at last.

"Lear, my darling, would you like to visit the Earl and Countess of Woden while their son is away in the West?" she asked him, hoping for a respite.

"I would like that exceedingly well", piped her son. Nurse Daphne sighed as she hated traveling but knew that the Woden's had no nurse. Lear was very excited and helped himself to a handful of crudite while his redoubtable nurse packed a few things in a small trunk. A messenger was sent on ahead to Countess Anca who felt very conscious of the honour although when Prince Lear arrived he was missing his mama for the first few days. But he quickly settled in and enjoyed playing with the other boys in Woden's entourage. With them he was just an ordinary boy albeit with an extraordinary talent for inventing new games and pastimes. When Brava arrived home from the Western Lands, he saw to it that young Lear was kitted out with a good, steady pony.

"It's quite pleasant to have him around", remarked Brava to his father the Earl. "But I may have to return to the West and I thought I'd visit the brothers in Ceredigion to see how they're coping with the pedlar's sentence".

"It's high time we thought about finding you a wife", asserted the Earl, "someone from the nobility. Have you met anyone?"

"There is a very regal lady of East Ceredigion", confided Brava, "but she wanted me to convert to the new Faith. I can gain instruction from the brothers but would you welcome her into our family?"

The Earl of Woden was agreeably surprised but said he must consult his Countess. Brava shook his father's hand then mounted his horse for the ride to Ceredigion.

Episode 3 A Bride for Brava

The Lady Merionydd lived in a stone longhouse with her parents and was deemed to be the County beauty. Brava had been visiting her family for a while and now told her father, the Squire, that he was exploring the new Faith with the brothers of Fairest Isle. Sir Gledwin Pryce loved Brava as a son yet deplored the old ways, as an adult convertee he had very determined ideas as to how things should be done and was most strong in faith. He enjoyed family prayers each day, had a fine, sonorous singing voice and led his household in rigorous debates on the new religion that had swept in from Ireland.

"I would like my only daughter to be married in a stone church with a holy man celebrating and my finest bugler to welcome us to the altar", he explained to Brava. Brava was invited to dine at the longhouse where Sir Gledwin entertained his guests and retinue. The young man sat between his future father-in-law and his bride to be. The Lady Merionydd wore her long, black hair plaited and wound around her head with a simple wild orchid by way of adornment. Her robe and cloak were woven of traditional Celtic tapestry of finest wool but she explained to Brava that her pure, white blouse was made of linen that he'd brought back from Ireland.

Merionydd was very interested in the new trade deal that Queen Athelstan was broaching with Sir Gledwin and other Western leaders.

"We have almost been annihilated by pestilence and disease", she said, "I am not old enough to remember the wars with the late King Wolfric but our Celtic bards still sing of the terrible fighting and death. I am not squeamish, I have tended the sick but talk to me about life".

Brava brought her a bowl of fruit and spoke about his parents. Then he told her of the fabulous tapestry hanging in an ancient, wooden temple to pagan gods. He was curious to learn more about this interesting young woman and asked her if he could order a portrait to be painted for a new tapestry that would adorn their future marital home. To his delight she was thrilled with this idea and consented to ride on horseback to meet the Earl and Countess at Woden's Dyke. As they talked, the rain poured down onto the slate roof of Gledwin's longhouse and Merionydd spoke again.

"Before we set out for Woden's Dyke, would you ride with my father to the slate quarries of the north? The quarry workers are asking their overlords for better pay which affects us directly as it puts up the price of our building materials. Father is hot-tempered and won't be lectured by his women folk. We can't afford what they are asking as the pestilence has attacked our crops. Your name is respected in this area, the people favour our nuptials, perhaps you could talk to their leaders". Brava consented then wrote home to his father the Earl to say that the whole Western area was struggling with the disease amongst the wheat but that talks had been put in place to find a solution.

"It's a conundrum", wrote Brava "that rich and poor alike eat bread and succumb to sickness and disease. Pestilence is no respecter of rank or person, old age happens to us all and death is inescapable. But the life expectancy of some is unfairly cut short and more needs to be done. I feel we must be supportive of Queen Athelstan's mission and I introduce to you my future wife who you will meet in one full moon from now".

"We have consented to this marriage with joy", said the Earl to his wife, "but I barely know my own son. He has grown taller than I in more ways than just physicality; the young lady seems very thoughtful and it's a marriage of true minds. But a stone church Anca?"

"Well they are young", replied his wife, "bit I will have to cover my head whereas you need to take your helmet off. Does that make any sense to you?"

"None at all", grumbled Woden, "but they always did have strange customs further west".

VII.   Wedded Bliss

Episode 1 - Rejoice, Renew

News that there would be a wedding in Ceredigion reached Queen Athelstan at her chamber. Nurse Daphne had returned from Woden's Dyke with the young Prince Lear who had been allowed to bring his new pony to the palace stables.

"Such a jolting as we've had", cried the redoubtable nurse. "I'm shaken to pieces, the roads to Woden's Dyke are in a parlous state with muddy potholes deep enough to drown in. What a relief to be home and dry. Your Grace shall I put the kettle on?"

The Queen consented then listened patiently as young Lear spoke of his pony and all his friends in the Earl of Woden's train.

"Mama", he cried with his sturdy legs apart and his hand on his hip, "I would like to go to the wedding to see the Celtic bride. Do they really have horns on their heads and live in caves?"

"No, my love, the horn is a golden circlet and Lady Merionydd lives in a longhouse built of stone with a slate roof", answered his mama, "but now you are home we have an even bigger surprise. Teacher Arasmus will be giving you lessons in Kingsmanship and statecraft, won't that be exciting?"

"We are exceedingly pleased", announced young Lear, "but is it true that Arasmus is from a star?"

"No, my child, he is from a big city where clever people learn to teach. I am sure you will enjoy meeting him". Then Nurse Daphne prepared the evening meal and grown up Jeremy the bard was admitted to play cheerful airs until bedtime.

When Prince Lear had settled in his own room the bard asked Queen Athelstan if she would like to choose a melody.

"I liked the song you wrote very much", she replied after much consideration, "but the tapestry reminds me of the past which is dead and gone. Have you perhaps another tune that celebrates the present?" The bard took up his lute and improvised a song on the spot about a poor man who wooed and won a great lady of much higher estate. The song told of daring deeds in the battlefield but a softening of old ways thanks to womanly advice. Queen Athelstan shed tears at the song then rose from her couch and put her hands together.

"Jeremy I would love to travel", she announced, taking him completely by surprise. The bard put down his lute and held her in his arms.

"My dear", he said very gently, "our first port of call must be Ceredigion for the wedding of Brava and Merionydd. But if you would like to go further we can set sail beyond Ireland to a totally different adventure from any of our forebears".

"You are a poet, songster and dreamer of dreams", sighed Athelstan, "we may fall off the end of the world into an unknown void but at least we'll be together".

Episode 2 - A Voyage of Joy

Captain O'Driscoll had been looking forward to his pie and pint of ale with the good landlady at his lodgings down at Broad Quay.

"No rest for the wicked", chortled the old lady as a messenger appeared announcing that the

Dowager Queen was planning to set sail beyond Ireland. The captain held his steak knife mid air and gaped open mouthed at the young lad before him.

"'Tis mortal unlucky to take a woman on board ship", the young man pronounced fatalistically. "But she pays a sovereign up front with another on arrival".

"On arrival", mused O'Driscoll, "there's nothing out there, just an abyss. She'll be fodder for the wild animals. She's bringing her bard you say? He'll have to be confined to barracks, I can't stick noise when I'm working. Well, ho hum, tell your mistress I accept. We'll sail around the coast tomorrow then after that it will depend on the wind. Right mate, I'm up for it". He finished his pie and pint, saluted his landlady, then went to prepare his ship for months at sea.

The wedding of Brava and Merionydd was a very simple affair but Queen Athelstan was moved to joyful tears, describing the bride as regal and gracious. Jeremy the bard played on his harp then the band struck up for dancing throughout the night as the older people drank a toast to the newlyweds. Bread was in short supply but on the coast, a harvest of oats had been plentiful, so Sir Gledwin ordered oat biscuits with local honey and there was a supply of fresh eggs with western strawberries smothered in clotted cream. Young Prince Lear wore his smartest royal tunic with the ensign of King Wolfric's house embroidered on his chest. But as the feasting neared dawn, the Queen and her bard slipped away from the rejoicing to ride on horseback to the harbour where their ship awaited them. Only Nurse Daphne saw them go as she prepared the young heir to the throne for bed.

"From here on in Jeremy, I am no longer your queen", said Athelstan to her bard. "You don't need to stand on ceremony, you can call me Athelstan or Thell for short and we'll just be an ordinary couple as we voyage to lands overseas". Captain O'Driscoll gave orders for the sails to be unfurled then the anchor was raised and slowly but surely the wooden and leather ship "The Countess Anca" moved out of harbour at West Ceredigion to tack around the Irish coast, heading for the unknown.

"Has this voyage ever been attempted before?" Jeremy asked the Captain.

"There are myths and legends in abundance", was the intriguing reply, "talk of mammoth beasts that float and people of a different tongue. We know that a crew of sailors and brothers attempted the voyage many years ago and lived to tell the tale. They spoke of an island amid endless ocean then strange trees, taller than the temples back home but it was unpopulated and they turned back. Is the lady alright or did she feel queasy?"

"I'm enjoying it", announced Athelstan appearing on deck, "I can see Ireland just disappearing into the distance".

"We must drop down a depth charge", explained O'Driscoll, "then lower the anchor for the night. You'll sleep well after days at sea".

Episode 3   Building a Longhouse

At East Ceredigion, Brava and Merionydd were taken in a wagon pulled by a pair of white horses to view their new home. The traditional Celtic longhouse had been built by freemen using local granite in a loose, dry stone fashion but inside, the new tapestry stitched with the young couple's portraits, stopped much of the draughts from the bay. From their main parlour they could see the waves rolling onto the shore and hear the curlews calling.

"On a clear day you can see Fairest Isle to the west and even Ireland sometimes", Sir Gledwin was pleased at their obvious delight then spoke to his manservant about bringing in some furnishings and a gift from Athelstan of an eiderdown.

Brava took his new wife Merionydd for many walks exploring the coast and also the mainland. They climbed the nearby highest point where a Celtic stone cross had been built to mark the passing of local mariners and seafarers in all the storms that part of the coast was prone to.

"I wonder where Athelstan and her bard are right now and how they're feeling?" Merionydd mused contentedly.

"Brave, pioneering or foolhardy? We may never find out my dear", answered Brava, handing her an interesting pebble. "My mother believes it's a whim of the queen's born out of boredom and fatigue but I think they will have wonderful adventures and I wondered if you would like to see Ireland if we can use the ship on their return? I am hoping they will come back".

"Yes, I really would like that. How did you get on with the quarry owners and their men?"

Brava sat on a rock and spread his cloak for her to join him. He explained that the workers had been given half of what they asked for to keep costs down but he had tried to persuade the profiteering owners not to pass on this extra expense to the buyers of the slate.

"It's tricky", said the young man, "because everyone is finding it hard now that there is contagion in the wheat. It has a knock on effect throughout the supply chain but the workers are hungry and complain that the price of oats has been sent artificially high".

"But my father speaks of some good news over in Glamorgan, he says that their wheat is now growing true after a series of storms that destroyed the diseased crops. He says that they are bringing grain to the mart, so we are hoping that we can sow seeds again and have good, new bread at last". Merionydd had a clear understanding of the problem and Brava was delighted with this last speech of hers.

"It's all good then", he said, then as the sun began to set they returned to their new home for an evening meal and Brava tended on their horses.

VIII.   Countess Anca

Episode 1   A Woollen Mill

In the absence of Queen Athelstan, the Earl and Countess of Woden travelled again to the west to set up trade deals in line with the queen's wishes. With the golden sovereign they bought bales of finest Celtic wool and it was sent by road home to Woden's Dyke where Anca's team of skilled seamstresses made floor to ceiling tapestries to sell back. But the sheep farmers on the Earl's land came in a body to complain that their wool was now classed as inferior to the Celtic wool and was now deemed only good enough to trade with the Irish. Suddenly these luxury tapestries became highly sought after by the gentry on both sides of the border.

"We still make tunics and tapestries with local wool", the Earl grew tired of explaining, "but the Celts pay with their own gold and the extra wealth benefits everybody. Anyone seeking a franchise in the business is welcome to apply, but it does entail a lot of travel. We are spending some of the money on improving roads in the area and I hope to build another ship to replace the missing one that appears lost at sea".

"We're having fun and making money", said Anca to her husband, "but the farmers have a point. We need to promote local produce as well but in our area it's more meat being sold than wool. Now some citizens are up in arms because they are asking for a share of the bounty, it's becoming a headache with seamstresses calling for payment in Celtic gold".

The Earl laughed out loud, "it's gone up in price but there is a very small supply yet to be smelted and more being mined. It's a gold mine, no pun intended".

"I need to visit the woollen mill to supervise the essential dying of the spun yarn with our local pigments. We have some glorious shades that local producers want the Celts to try, maybe the local farmers will be appeased by this as the gentian blue and vermilion red are grown at Woden's Dyke". The Countess explained this process to her husband and his delight was evident, he said that it was worth opening a cask of ale for and he penned a short letter on vellum to his son in the west to advise him of all these latest developments.

Brava showed the letter to his Celtic wife Merionydd, but she asked if they could go inland to the fields of her country to buy good wheat. She was more concerned with getting her workers fed and expressed regret that so much Celtic gold was leaving their country for Woden's Dyke. Her husband burned the letter, decided not to answer it, then rode with Merionydd to the mart in Glamorgan to buy grain to store in their barn at East Ceredigion.

"We will one day inherit the Earl's title and lands, then the gold can be restored but the business is thriving and Woden's Dyke suddenly very wealthy", Brava pleaded with his wife.

"I know, it's wonderful", she answered, "but money is useless when people are sick and the contagion is in the wheat. There is a time to sow and a time to reap, we need to get this good grain planted before the rains come then there will be rejoicing at next year's harvest".

Episode 2. Freedom Forever

The ship "Countess Anca" was sailing full west, with the lookout man at the top of the mast praying earnestly for a sighting of land on the horizon. He had cramp from sitting so long as he clutched the wooden mast but after months at sea, with salt beef and fresh water rations running low, he spied what he sought.

"Land ahoy", he yelled, and he slid swiftly down to speak with his captain of the coast he saw in the distance. "There are blue hills far yonder", cried the lookout man to the assembled company, his wide eyes blazing. "Then there is a mighty waterfall, clean and fresh, tumbling between rocks to the golden, sandy beach. The shallow salt waters are as full of fish as I have ever seen with strange flowers at the edge of the sand dunes further inland".

Captain O' Driscoll steered the ship towards the natural harbour then ordered the anchor to be lowered and reviewed his armoury of swords.

"We should be armed", he advised his crew and guests, "we don't know if there are people or if they are hostile. Miss Athelstan, would you like to go ashore with your companion?" The queen assented but asked if she could take a short dagger in case of need, she was not afraid she said but this was a precaution.

Once ashore, the ship's company filled all their empty wooden barrels with fresh water from the natural stream beneath the waterfall. Some local, indigenous people saw them from behind the sand dunes but kept their distance. They smiled and talked amongst themselves but Captain

O'Driscoll advised his men not to show any sign that might be seen as aggressive.

Athelstan took the catch of fish from her crew and salted it as she had once been taught before her first marriage. She prepared each fish then laid them out to dry in the sun on a fallen tree trunk. The local people retreated through the inland woods so Jeremy and the captain loaded all the water and salt fish onto boats to take it all back for storage in the hold of the Countess Anca.

"We could explore further along the coast", suggested Jeremy but the sailors grumbled at this and after consideration, Athelstan said she felt they'd seen enough and perhaps should head for home.

"My son will be growing up fast and we must organise his coronation. Nurse Daphne is no longer young and my tally of marks on my pocket book suggests we have been away two years and one month. Do the winds favour us Captain?"

"Indeed they do", replied O'Driscoll, "it's a fair breeze that will blow us straight to port at Fishguard Harbour then it's a day's ride to Woden's Dyke. It's always quicker homeward bound".

Episode 3   Wisdom Prevails

Back home at the royal palace, Tutor Arasmus was instructing Prince Lear in modern history. They were studying ancient vellum documents of the wars between Lear's grandfather, King Wolfric, and the Celts across the border to the west. Then, Arasmus explained the complexities of the new trade deals organised by the Earl and Countess of Woden.

"I admit I wouldn't want to fight", declared the younger man, "but what became of the travelling rogue who murdered my sister?"

"He lives but under house arrest with a community of brothers who curtail his freedom", answered the Tutor, "I am sorry you have been told this story, it doesn't seem right to me, it was all before you were born and the pedlar is so distressed in his mind it was said he knew not what he did".

Lear considered this then looked again at the ancient documents.

"I will be a just and merciful king, Teacher", said Lear. "It seems to me that the Earl is much influenced by his son and the Celtic bride. Perhaps like us the Celts are finding war too costly in money as well as manpower. Can we talk about the problem with their wheat? I hear they're having to eat oats and honey". The tutor was very pleased to talk about a topical, less dangerous subject so he explained how the storms had left the lands fallow but good, disease free wheat was sown after and now the Celts were eating new bread once more.

"That's all for today's lesson", he finished, "will you exercise your horses now?" So Lear went out into the sunshine to do just that.

IX.   A Homecoming

Episode 1. Souvenir of Travel

The anchor was raised, all the ship's company set to the oars to row the ship the Countess Anca out of New Harbour, and Captain O'Driscoll finally gave Jeremy the bard permission to sing sea shanties to motivate the men.

"Heave ho! Heave ho!" Sang the men as Athelstan looked her last at the new country they had all discovered.

The phases of the moon seemed to pass very quickly on the journey home to Fishguard Harbour as Athelstan kept a tally of each passing day using vellum, a quill and a gall for ink that the captain had found below deck. Jeremy improvised songs and ballads using the lute he'd brought with him, keeping everyone's spirits high, as the wind blew steadily towards the east.

"Land ahoy", was once again the long awaited cry as the keen sighted lookout man came down from his eyrie to speak of a channel between cliffs topped with grass and low vegetation. Captain O'Driscoll ordered the men to row upstream and now they all recognised the Celtic village of Fishguard where a stout Nurse Daphne was waving a banner with a young man beside her.

"How did they know? We have been away for four years and two months", exclaimed the queen but the captain suggested that Arasmus had read the stars. Indeed there he was, standing behind his student, a young and vigorous Prince Lear.

"My son, I am old now", declared Athelstan, "but you must now be king. We will hold your coronation in a stone building and give thanks for all that you are. Nurse Daphne you will be well rewarded for all the time and energy you have dispensed, we thank you fully for your services". Nurse Daphne curtsied to the queen and shed a joyful tear.

"Such a happy homecoming", she uttered as Jeremy the bard bowed low to his new monarch then invited Captain O'Driscoll to come forward and be presented to the king.

Episode 2. Festival Fever

Jeremy the bard was in his element and enjoying himself hugely as he rushed from here to there organising a big, celebratory festival for the new king. Bards came from far and wide bringing new ideas, strange musical instruments and lyrical poetry as King Lear loved literature and song. There was a role for Tutor Arasmus who was writing an epic poem about the wars with the west and how Bladud and his successors had brought peace to English and Celtic lands. Lear himself had promised to learn to play the lute in readiness for a special concert with the Queen Mother in attendance.

As the festival preparations continued, all the pages put up the great marquees and set out wooden benches for all to enjoy the fun. There was to be a banquet for everyone who could get there with stalls serving bread, cheese and meat pasties but also honey cakes, ale and wine.

"Brava and Merionydd have sent word of their apologies", said a disappointed Lear to his mother. "They gave no reason except to say that the journey would be too much for them at this time".

Athelstan shrugged her shoulders and continued with organising the spice cabinet for the cooks. She had not seen the Earl or his wife Anca at all since her return from overseas and was too wrapt up in her new life with Jeremy and also in looking forward to the coronation of her son. But Woden's Dyke was also celebrating the new king and finally announced that the Celtic bride was expecting a child.

"So my old, never sought love is to be a grandsire," said Athelstan, "such a relief I didn't end up as his wife". Then she went to the chamber of her long serving Nurse Daphne to take her spiced cakes and fruit wine as a special treat.

Episode 3   King Lear Inherits

After weeks of preparation the coronation of the young king was a polished ceremony of music and ritual. At the command of King Lear his crown was of Celtic gold with jewels and semi precious stones garnered from across the realm. He decided to set a new tradition by mounting his horse and addressing the common people gathered outside the royal palace. He stood in the stirrups to project his voice to the throng, proclaiming peace, prosperity and justice for all. His former tutor Arasmus quietly asked his mentor the Earl of Woden if he could now retire from active duty then slipped away from the feasting and noise to join his own friends leaving for the coast and Fairest Isle.

The brothers welcomed Arasmus to their community but Brother Libris confessed that Cennen the travelling pedlar had grown stronger under their care, making a perilous crossing to the mainland of West Ceredigion in a small boat and none knew what had become of him.

"But he is old now", said the brother, "and we feel he poses no risk".

So King Lear settled to the business of ruling and his mother retired once again from public duty as Jeremy the bard talked endlessly of a special tour of the whole realm.

Printed in Great Britain
by Amazon

87717653R00031